Clarion Books
a Houghton Mifflin Company imprint
215 Park Avenue South, New York, NY 10003
Text copyright © 2005 by Linda Sue Park
Illustrations copyright © 2005 by Maggie Smith

The illustrations were executed in watercolor and pencil.
The text was set in 24-point Cantoria.

www.houghtonmifflinbooks.com

Printed in the U.S.A.

Library of Congress Cataloging-in-Publication Data
Park, Linda Sue.
What does Bunny see? : a book of colors and flowers / by Linda Sue Park ;
pictures by Maggie Smith.
p. cm.
Summary: A rabbit wanders through the various flowers and colors of a cottage garden.
ISBN 0-618-23485-3
[1. Color—Fiction. 2. Flowers—Fiction. 3. Rabbits—Fiction.
4. Gardens—Fiction. 5. Stories in rhyme.] I. Smith, Maggie, ill. II. Title.
PZ8.3.P1637Wh 2005   [E]—dc22   2004012312

ISBN-13: 978-0-618-23485-1
ISBN-10: 0-618-23485-3

WOZ 10 9 8 7 6 5 4 3 2 1

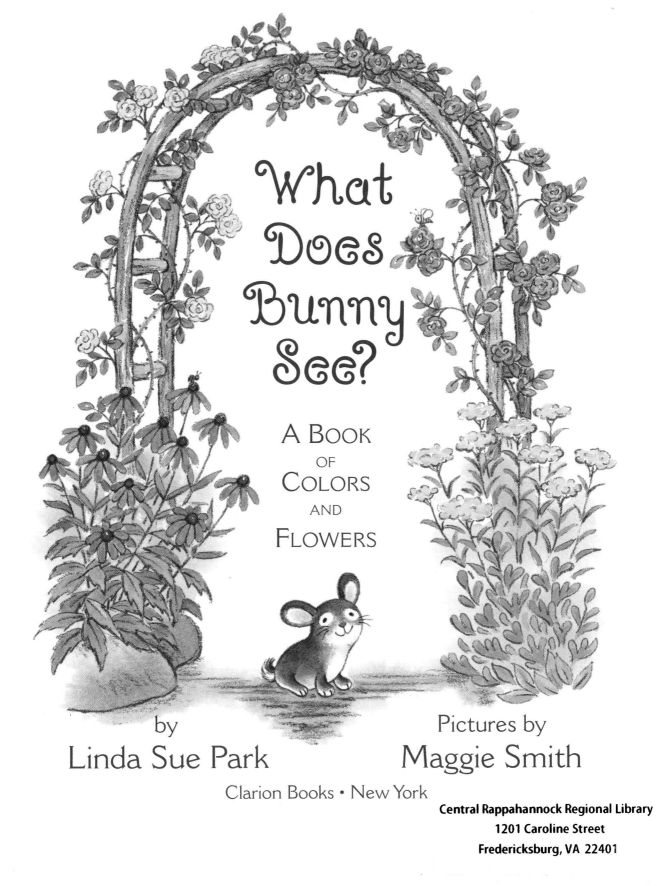

What Does Bunny See?

A BOOK
OF
COLORS
AND
FLOWERS

by
Linda Sue Park

Pictures by
Maggie Smith

Clarion Books • New York

To Eve and Anna Botelho
—L.S.P.

For Lucy Jane Maguire

—xoxo, M.S.

In a cottage garden
flowers in their beds
Bunny hopping down the path
what she sees is—

red!

Blushing scarlet poppies bloom
just above her head.

In a cottage garden
past the pussy willow
Bunny nibbles tender shoots
what she sees is—

10

yellow!

Primroses are nestled low
in their leafy pillows.

In a cottage garden
hear the water burble
Bunny drinking from the stream
what she sees is—

13

purple!

Violets nod their heads in time
to the songbird's warble.

16

In a cottage garden
ears and whiskers clean
Bunny finds a patch of lawn
what she sees is—

green!

Grass is growing lushly
with clover in between.

In a cottage garden
plip and *plop* and *plink!*
Bunny freezes, twitching nose
what she sees is—

pink!

Water lily landing pad
and bulging eyes that blink.

In a cottage garden
peeping from below
Bunny sees a cheerful color
that begins with O—

orange!

Freckled tiger lilies dance
putting on a show.

In a cottage garden
can she wiggle through?
Bunny digging by the fence
what she sees is—

blue!

Morning glories yawning wide
Bunny's yawning too.

31

In a nest of grasses
snuggled warm and tight
Bunny dreams a rainbow dream
colors blossom-bright.